AN

WITH A CRIMINAL KISS

JERI CAIN ROSSI

CREATION BOOKS

INTERNATIONAL

Angel With A Criminal Kiss
Jeri Cain Rossi
A Creation Book
ISBN 1 871592 45 3
Copyright © Jeri Cain Rossi 1989, 1996
All world rights reserved
Edited by Dave Cappello
First published 1996
Creation Books
83 Clerkenwell Road
London EC1R 5AR, UK
Cover illustration:
Joe Coleman
Photograph of Jeri Cain Rossi by:
Tessa Hughes-Freeland
An earlier version of Part One,
Angel With A Criminal Kiss,
was originally published in 1989
by Primal Publishing, Allston, Massachusetts
Design and typesetting:
Bradley Davis, PCP International
Author's acknowledgements:
Deepest gratitude to all my dear friends who lent me
money, fed me, bought me drinks and cared for me.
Special thanks to Jack Sargeant, James and Peter at
Creation, Dave Cappello, Duane Davis, Joe Coleman,
Vicki Archambault, Michael McInnis, Big Rus, Vanessa
Skantze, Nick Zedd, Tessa Hughes-Freeland,
and my family.

Contents

ONE:
ANGEL WITH A CRIMINAL KISS

TWO:
WELCOME TO THE LAND OF THE DROWNED

Contents

ANGEL
WITH A CRIMINAL KISS

And Other Stories

Mortal love never worked out for me,
but I make an exception in your case.

Part One

ANGEL
WITH A CRIMINAL KISS

Carrying The Cross

She came alone.

She came dressed like a French queen from the 18th century, it being Halloween. The party was already wild and loud, and she was chatting it up with a ghost when John showed up. He didn't wear a mask and it scared her.

Then she saw the cunt on his arm. The cunt he left her for. Her heart sank pretty low about this. She couldn't stop putting shots of Jim Beam to her mouth and pulling the trigger. It took every ounce of restraint not to look at them.

Soon the liquor numbed her into a kind of crumbling wall. She fell on the couch and stayed there. She forgot to talk when people chattered at her. She listened to them and answered them, only she forgot to use her throat. They left her alone.

John and his cunt left after a couple of hours hand in hand. The hosts were picking up bottles and cans and hinting that maybe the party was over when she decided that it was time for the queen to walk home.

She stepped off the curb and headed east on Colfax. One foot and then another foot. She was drunk out of her skull and it was like walking on a tightrope and not caring if there was a safety net. One foot, another foot.

"Excuse me miss." She found herself sitting on a bus stop bench crying when she looked up.

"Excuse me miss, may I sit with you?" By his accent she figured he was Haitian.

"No you may not seet with me," she said and got up and staggered defiantly the wrong way home.

He followed her down the sidewalk. She turned around. "What are you, a trick or a treat?" she said nastily.

"Miss miss I pay you please. You are very pretty miss," he said standing very close to her.

She laughed bitterly. "You must be a trick."

He took her hand and pointed at the apartment house across the street. "Come this way miss please."

She was drunk enough to be annoyed and curious at the same time. She thought about John and that cunt all over each other in the corner of the kitchen at the party.

He'll come back to me, she thought. He was just showing off. He'll call me tomorrow and we'll have a big laugh about it and then he'll come over and we'll fuck our brains out like before. She crossed the street. One foot, another foot.

In the light of the stairwell, the Haitian was uglier than she could have imagined, not to mention that he had a sizeable pot belly. The stairwell stank like a decade of piss. They climbed two flights.

It was a ratty one bedroom apartment. Five Haitians were sleeping on the floor. They awoke and stared her up and down. She took one look at the situation and ducked into the bathroom.

She sat on the toilet and bent over her lap, her head spinning. Down the hall, the Haitians prepared the only bedroom for their buddy's night of entertainment. By the tone of their high-pitched, rapid-fire French patois, the roommates were as excited as he was about his purchase.

She tried to focus. A legion of roaches strolled on the floor on the pipes on the wall on the ceiling on the sink on the towels on the tub. She panicked, John I love you come back come back save me I'm dying without you.

She rose from the toilet and nudged the door open. The Haitians were still in the bedroom preparing the bed. She took two steps down the hall and was out the door and hurried down the stairwell out to the street. She ran up the block and made a turn.

She was quickly sobering and thinking what a stupid stunt that was. She'd have to call John and tell him all about it, and was laughing hysterically at herself, when he caught up with her.

"Where are you going, miss?" he said and politely took her by the arm.

"Look asshole. I'm Marie Antoinette and I'm going home. You didn't even pay me first, you worm. I'm supposed to get paid first. I don't even think you have any money." She teetered on the tightrope. She was going to fall.

"I want everything in your wallet, you pathetic ugly fuckhead." She thrust her open palm in his face.

He reluctantly reached for his wallet and pulled out 60 dollars. "Here you are miss. I have no more. I am lonely, please." She took the money and blankly stared at it in her hand.

He led her back to the apartment house. Up two flights, into the room, and closed the door.

Like A Francis Bacon Painting

It was 1923. Her hair was big and red. She had the biggest teeth he ever saw. He fell in love and they got married. It lasted 37 years.

They were rebels. They were libertines. They fed on the perverse like vampires. Tangiers, Paris, Singapore, Mexico City. Narcotics. Loose sex. Living on the fringe. Down on the law.

Then he died of emphysema. And she could not handle being 65 anymore, at least not without a playmate.

So she parked the Cadillac on the Peoria Bridge and descended into the smelly baptism of the Illinois River. She bobbed up and down, big and red like a buoy until a fisherman noticed her and called the Coast Guard.

For a week she sat in the psychiatric wing and

pouted.

Two days after she was released she drove back to the bridge and jumped again.

She made it.

Going Nowhere Fast

Dean had a black '73 Plymouth Fury with red interior and a magnetic plastic Mary on the dash. He wore a holster loaded with a pint of Jack in a silver decanter engraved with the words *Bourbon Cowboy*.

He surveyed the herd of partygoers at a loft on Thayer Street and moved in on a pretty roan filly, Charlene, a poetess. They got drunk and drunker killing their idols and making fun of art school and art students in general. Dean sweet-talked Charlene into the Fury and they dashed off to Lowell, thirty miles away, to desecrate Kerouac's grave.

Somebody had left a bottle of Night Train next to the stone. The two drank it dry and got sick. How did those old farts drink that piss? Then they irreverently fucked under the same moon and stars that Rimbaud had fucked under and that made them sicker. So sick, that on the way back to Boston they had to pull off the highway to find a diner to drink coffee and smoke cigarettes until the sun rose and their bellies set.

They crashed at Dean's loft until nine o'clock that evening. Charlene made enchiladas and they washed them down with tequila shots. Matthew came over and sold them crystal meth, which wasn't very good but it got them going at least. They all went down to Foley's and drank dollar shots and watched television.

A drunken, smelly street lady wouldn't stop intruding on their booth so Dean coaxed her into doing a striptease. She pulled off her blouse for three dollars to expose a black brassiere and a hideous tattoo of a frog on her left breast. Off came the brassiere and her sagging breasts went loose every which way. She had her slacks, no panties, down around her knees before the barkeep rushed over angrily and threw them all out.

Dean and Matthew ran off to the liquor store before it closed. Charlene took a cab home and wrote a poem about drag racing.

Nameless Fuck

It was in some bar in North Miami. She put four quarters in the jukebox to hear ten songs she totally hated by stupid people like Bob Seeger and Jimmy Buffett. Then she proceeded to drink. Black Russians. And she began to think pretentious thoughts like how gifted an artist she was and wasn't she decadent to pick out this obvious white trash waterhole to get drunk at today.

She was furiously drinking and writing in a black book when a pitcher of beer landed on her table and asked to sit down. Her first reaction was to flick the fly away. No man she met here could be of any use to her, no how no way. She motioned for him to sit.

His name was Tom, Dick and Harry and he lived in Florida all his life and had a police record and sometimes worked construction and would she like to come over to his mobile home to party?

She didn't like to admit it aloud but she got a sick pleasure out of occasionally allowing some stupid dick to pick her up, then totally ridiculing him as the evening degenerates. The dick never catches on because he's so stupid and boring.

But after five Black Russians and three glasses of syrupy Budweisers he sort of looked like Willem Dafoe. And he lit every cigarette she pulled out like a gentleman. And he reminded her of a character out of a Sam Shepard play.

They pushed 90 mph in his Trans Am to his trailer. He got right down to business. He made her suck his cock forever. Then he pulled up her skirt and ripped open her pantyhose and rammed it in. He came and the whole trailer park heard about it.

She woke up about noon. The thing sleeping next to her totally repulsed her. The more she remembered about the last evening, the sicker she got. She looked around. The place was totally tacky. Crushed-velvet furniture and shag carpet. Then she noticed that her pantyhose were totally destroyed and her diaphragm was still in her purse.

She got up and washed her face, then started the 20 mile or so walk back to town.

Four-Foot Itch

Little Tommy jumped off the kitchen chair and waddled to the refrigerator. He grabbed the handle, opened it and reached for a bottle of beer. Then he wobbled into the living room and hopped up on the couch. He felt under the cushion and brought out one of the assorted magazines he had hidden there.

A pictorial essay entitled *Girls Who Eat Cum* inspired Tommy to unzip his slacks and rub himself. Within three minutes he finished. Then he began to cry. A grown man, 36 years old, and he had never jacked-off into anything besides his hand. He drank the rest of the beer, which got him staggering around his apartment.

Tommy had reached the point in the evening which turned into despair and had to be slept off immediately. That's when he heard the explosion of harsh arguing through the wall from the apartment next door.

Tommy cupped his fat little hand to his wee little ear against the wall.

It happened very fast. Four minutes maximum. The high-pitched feminine threats. The low-pitched masculine sarcasm. Flesh being pulverized. The feminine threats turning into terror. Glass breaking. Furniture scraping on the floor.

Something gurgling. Door opens. Fast footsteps on the back stairwell. Then, nothing. Tommy hobbled to a window to see a dark Plymouth gun down the street. He unlocked his back door and tippytoed into the next apartment.

She was laying right there on the kitchen floor. Her neck didn't look right. But she was very pretty. An artist or something. The place reeked of turpentine and there were canvases stacked everywhere. He moved closer and noticed that the black slip she wore was torn and she had no panties on.

Tommy had never seen a woman's pussy in the flesh before. He stared at it for a long time. He studied the blonde pubic hair. Then he pushed the legs apart and peered in. It didn't look real. He touched it. He put his finger in it as deep as he could then examined the finger. He smelled it. It smelled of perfume. Then he put his whole hand in it. His groin began to itch and throb. His whole body itched. One big itch.

He quickly wiggled back to his apartment, locked the door and jacked-off into the hand that he had investigated the dead girl with.

Then he took a shower and went to bed.

Sloe Gin And Fast Pussy

He liked brunettes. He liked blondes. But Dean especially liked redheads. Red as Hell redheads. He liked the way their skin was almost translucent. He liked the way they always had pretty fingers. And they had names like Suzanne and Camille and Margerite. Names like that turned him on. But most of all, redheads knew how to please a man. They knew how to fuck.

He liked fucking them in his Plymouth Fury. He liked taking them to some tourist-infested spot and fucking them in the parking lot. Like at a Celtics game. He hated basketball. He hated people who went to basketball games. But he loved to fuck redheads in his Fury in a crowded parking lot. He liked to hear ten thousand people cheer him slamming down her court. The redheads loved it, too. They always came back for more.

He loved to drink gin when he went out looking

for pussy. He liked bourbon, too. He even liked bourbon better, but bourbon made him mean. So did vodka. Brunettes and blondes fell for him when he was in bourbon mode. Gin, on the other hand, is redhead bait. He didn't know why. It just turned out that way. And it worked.

He kidnapped a willing, laughing redhead once. She didn't have anything better to do for spring break anyway. She studied sculpture, and Dean generally loathed art students, but made an exception in her case because he liked her hair and her laugh.

Dean used to live in Denver so they drove and laughed all the way to Colorado. They stayed at the Royal Host on Colfax near the capitol building in Denver for a full week. She paid for all the lodging and alcohol.

He showed her every flop-house where Neal Cassady lived in the '40s and she laughed. He showed her every art gallery and every strip joint and she laughed. She showed him every orifice in her body, laughing. He became annoyed at her laughing and made a few more orifices with a jack knife. She stopped laughing.

Dean got back to Boston on a Wednesday and slept until Friday afternoon. He cashed his unemployment check, paid rent on his loft, and bought a quart of gin for his liquor cabinet. The Fury was running like a charm.

The bomb hadn't dropped yet. And the sunset was looking cherry red.

The Flowers Must Be Punished

Three years they lived together. Kenny and Ladonna. One night Kenny looks up from dinner and tells Ladonna to get the hell out by tomorrow. Just like that. Like he was reading sports scores out loud. She looks at him and can't believe what she's hearing and laughs. He throws his plate of food at her and screams GET OUT OF MY SIGHT YOU STINKING CUNT.

Ladonna felt like she was watching all this on the television. WHAT IS THE MATTER WITH YOU? she yells back, shaking. WHAT BROUGHT THIS ON? AM I IMAGINING THIS? YOU SAID YOU'D LOVE ME FOREVER JUST LAST NIGHT WHEN WE HAD SEX.

Kenny looks at her like he's looking at something so loathsome that he can barely keep from spitting.

WHEN I SAID I CARED FOR YOU I MEANT THAT I LOATHED YOU. WHEN I SAID I LOVED YOU, I MEANT THAT I CAN'T STAND THE SIGHT OF YOU. YOU MAKE ME SICK. THE WAY YOU DO MY LAUNDRY AND COOK AND CLEAN. YOU'D DO ANYTHING FOR ME YOU MISERABLE CREATURE. I BET YOU'D EAT MY SHIT IF I ASKED YOU TO YOU MINDLESS SLOB. I CAN'T LOVE YOU UNLESS I CAN LOVE A TOILET BRUSH OR A MOP.

Ladonna left her body and ran to the bathroom. Kenny tackled her in the hall. He ripped her blouse open and bit down. He held down her arms with one hand and pushed up her skirt ripping her pantyhose with the other. He unzipped his trousers then nudged her thighs apart. Kenny entered her like a demolition derby. Ladonna laid there like a sidewalk. Their trailer shook.

Mrs. Rose slid open her kitchen window. She leaned her head out sideways as much as possible to hear everything. Those nasty people next door were going straight to Hell. She was sure.

No Plot But Lots
Of Action

He bought a quart of beer and two shot bottles of Jack and stashed them in her purse. They entered the theater for the Russ Meyer double feature. Both flicks were really Bad, but they were sick and sleazy and violent. This made them Good and the booze made them Brilliant.

Four and a half hours later they stumbled out of the theater into twilight and immediately headed for a liquor store to pick up more Jack and cigarettes. They walked three blocks to her rooming house.

Scene one. Low budget and to the point. Took about fifteen minutes to climax.

Scene two. She came out behind the screen in seamed pantyhose and danced lewdly. He grabbed her and ripped apart the pantyhose and stuck it in. Two minutes.

Scene three. He had to quit after twenty minutes. The booze was making him soft.

She staggered into the bathroom in the hallway and lit newspaper in the shower and watched it burn. The smoke alarm in the stairwell went off and the drug dealer, his bitch, the junkie couple and the alcoholic loner who also lived in the rooming house clamored angrily out of their rooms. The drug dealer ripped out the battery.

"Crazy white bitch."

Scene four. She came, kind of, almost. Maybe. Maybe not.

Scene five. They both had to quit and go to sleep. She dreamed of mutilating small animals. He didn't dream but tossed a lot.

Please Stay On The Earth, My Love

She tried again last night. Got too drunk and started knocking on Heaven's door. Eddie had to hold her down from crawling over the banister and jumping down the stairwell.

He loved her more than anything. His art, his life. And she kept trying to off herself.

It only happened when she drank. Didn't happen every time, either. Just like Russian roulette, you never knew when the bullet hit until it did.

But today, the day after, she was calm as a kitten, as always, after sticking her head into the demon's mouth.

His head whirled with troubled thoughts. He wanted to scream, he wanted to cry, he wanted to kill. He felt pathetic and helpless and trapped and wanted release from this sentence, or some kind of redemption. He wished they were strangers so he could walk away.

But he knew her whole story. Hell, he helped write seven of the chapters. He still needed to be her hero.

MY GOD GIRL. PLEASE LISTEN TO ME. DON'T DO THIS TO YOURSELF. I NEED YOU. YOU'RE MY MUSE BITCH. I DON'T WANT TO GROW OLD IN THIS STINKING WORLD WITHOUT YOU. DON'T FUCKING DIE ON ME YOU SMELLY CUNT.

She rolled over on her side away from him and mumbled. She did not awaken.

You're Always Alone

Maybe it didn't occur to her that it was an atrocity to lock her siren beauty inside her apartment for days at a time. Venturing out only well-covered. A scarf holding in her vanilla-colored hair. Sunglasses and gloves always. Even in scorching heat.

She routinely made three stops every Thursday: to the superette to have groceries delivered, to the pharmacy to buy toiletries and cosmetics, and to the liquor store to buy three quarts of tequila and margarita mix, also to be delivered.

He spied on her from the unit across the hall. He imagined all kinds of things about her. He imagined that she was a screen starlet in hiding, weary of the fast and shallow life. Tired of her beauty opening all the wrong doors.

Around noon she opened the door to pick up the

mail. Always junk mail. He would be waiting and studied her through his peephole. For those thirty seconds a day he waited.

He worked the three to eleven shift as a security guard at a hotel downtown. Sometimes he got so jealous. Thinking of her. Wondering what she was doing that very minute. She never had visitors that he knew of. But what if she did tonight while he was working? Maybe it would be an old lover, a handsome actor, he imagined, who would appear at her door, broken and begging for her forgiveness. And tears would come to her eyes and they would embrace. And he would whisper, let's go to Paris, darling, let's leave tonight, we'll send for your things when we get settled.

It was all he could do to contain himself on the bus ride home when he got this riled up. Her light was on, curtains closed. He waited. A shadow moved close to the curtain. He raced two steps at a time to the third floor and, holding in his gasps as much as possible, creeped to her door and listened. The hi-fi was on and a cupboard door slammed. She was alone. His heart sighed with temporary relief.

She poured the margarita mix in the blender along with ice and tequila. While it blended she salted the lip of a glass. Then she poured the mixture in. Frankie Laine crooned from the hi-fi. She smiled demurely in the direction of the music as she sipped the margarita. She moved toward the window and parted the curtain. The street was desolate except for him. He was still dressed in his security uniform and was pacing back and forth smoking a cigarette. He paused and looked up. She let go of the curtain and turned towards the hi-fi. You must leave now. My new young and handsome lover is waiting for me, she thought aloud, and the string section came on strong.

Ugly As A God

Vodka is a cruel drug. It makes you dispassionate. It makes you want to hurt back.

Dean decided after four vodkas that Norma Jean totally repulsed him. She was a grotesque performance artiste. A worthless piece of mankind. She thought she was so decadent. Waving her fat ass around. She thought she was God's gift to art and men. Somebody ought to give her back. He pushed her out the door of the bar towards his Plymouth Fury.

Norma Jean cheerfully chattered away about a goddess retreat she had recently attended when she asked Dean where they were going now. Dean slapped her hard on the mouth.

"I'm taking you to godhead, Norma Jean, now get into the car."

Stunned, Norma Jean paused, then opened the

passenger side door. She had met Dean at a poetry workshop a couple months earlier and was intrigued by his violent erotic imagery and surly manner. Besides, she had been wanting this fuck for a long time. He was too handsome. He looked like Montgomery Clift.

"Oh daddy, I feel so dirty."

"You're hideous and I am going to cleanse you, Norma Jean."

They drove up the mountain towards Mother Cabrini Shrine. Dean held on to Norma Jean's hair and sharply pushed her face in his lap the whole ride so he didn't have to hear her talk. He parked the car near the statue of Jesus and brought out clothes-line from the trunk.

"Strip, Norma Jean."

"Sure, daddy daddy daddy."

She took off her clothes, thinking nothing in particular, feeling totally secure. A real man at last. She'd had enough of flaccid art students.

He bound and gagged her to a tree. Then he lit a Pall Mall and looked down to the city lights. Three steps and he could be falling into its filth. Dean sucked the Pall Mall then burned it into Norma Jean's breast. She screamed through the gag. Then she giggled. He lit another cigarette and another then burned her again and again. Then he siphoned gas out of the car.

Norma Jean had maybe 36 welts. She was dripping with anticipation. This was going to be a good fuck. And the lights below were so beautiful. She rolled her hips and moaned, until Dean poured gasoline down upon her head. Her eyes stung and she choked.

"Norma Jean, I am going to cleanse you and you will thank me for it. I am going to make you beautiful."

He lit another Pall Mall and smoked it to the end. Then he lit Norma Jean.

She is looking good.

Dripping Pretty

Getting too close. Too close too close. Rip the skin off. Pull it off like a used condom. Flush it down the river. Wash it all away like a baptism. Hallelujah. Pure again. New start. Start again.

See a pretty girl on the street. It's hot. She's wearing a peach dress that swishes with her walk. She's got blonde hair and a red face. She's dripping with sweat. You let her pass by then pause and turn around and follow ten paces behind.

You match her pace for two stoplights. Her feet must hurt in those white high heels. You think maybe you're a pervert to follow her. That it's wrong. You think that somehow you're invading her privacy. You're not supposed to watch people this close. But nobody is watching you as far as you can tell. You're getting away with it. You feel bad but you can't help yourself.

She stops at a newsstand and buys a newspaper. You catch up and browse. She's putting off a scent. It's rolling off her skin. It chokes your lungs like a cockring. God you want to touch her peach dress. It looks like raw silk.

She turns and glances around as if her antenna picked something up. She scans you in a millionth of a second and has deemed you harmless and insignificant. She walks into the street. A Plymouth Fury gives a love call. It stops next to her. She laughs and opens the passenger door and slides in. You stand on the curb. The Fury peels away. Oil drips on the pavement.

You watch for a minute then go a Store 24 and buy a gallon of strawberry ice cream and eat it all watching television. It drips on the sheets sometimes.

Through The Eye
Of A Needle

Dean made the phone call to Lazlo to scout some powder. Lazlo was trying to kick it again and was drinking heavily but he had product to sell and invited Dean over. They were old shooting buddies from way back.

Juanita, Lazlo's wife, answered the door and almost fell on Dean, drunk. Lazlo was sitting on the living room sofa looking bleary-eyed holding a Black Label and his four-month-old son, Anthony. The television was on with the volume off. Anthony's volume turned up loud. Juanita handed Dean a beer and took Anthony screaming into the bedroom. Lazlo switched the channel to boxing. Dean hated watching sports but politely went through the motions. He finished his beer within five minutes. Lazlo yelled to Juanita to bring another. Juanita lay on the bed in the next room with Anthony, too drunk to move anymore. Lazlo suggested that he and Dean move to the kitchen. Then he brought out his rig and powder.

Dean's mouth watered at the sight of it. He had to start being cool. This was the third time this week. He'd be cool. Just not right now. He added a few drops of water to the powder in a bent, scorched tablespoon and melted the mixture over the stove.

Dean did his shot. Nice and slow. He knew how to shoot. Lazlo had so much fun watching that he could not resist and prepared a shot for himself.

Dean leaned back in the kitchen chair saint-like. The ceiling fan made a sound like wings flapping. Dean looked up and saw the Holy Ghost. The Holy Ghost looking down on Dean. Something sharp pushed through his hands and feet. Christ, it must have felt good.

"Jesus Christ, Dean!"

He looked down and saw Mary-John crying. Good Mary-John. Pure Mary-John. Mary-John who loved him. Mary-John who filled him with revulsion. He wanted to spit on Mary-John. He wanted to slap her shining face. He wanted to betray her even if she was the only mortal that cared about him. The luxury of it. It made him feel like a shithead and a godhead at the same time. Like an angel and a criminal. Cry all you want Mary-John, he thought in his glory.

Dean came out of his nod and looked over to Lazlo. He sat slumped over in the chair. Dean stared at him. It registered that something was not right. He reached over and tapped Lazlo's shoulder. Lazlo slipped unconscious onto the kitchen floor, the point still in his arm. Dean bent over Lazlo and shook him. He called out to Juanita but she was passed out or maybe Dean's lips weren't working. Lazlo's lips were definitely blue.

Dean panicked. He wondered if he should call Emergency. No, that would take two minutes and he didn't have two minutes. Then he thought that he was taking too long thinking about it. He began blowing and sucking into Lazlo's mouth. He never brought anyone back before. He pushed down hard on Lazlo's chest. You son of a bitch you asshole scum, he screamed at Lazlo's blue face. Dean got up to run away. Nausea forced him to the sink. He dry-heaved beer. Lazlo's dead. Lazlo's dead, he thought, but was too sick to care. Lazlo stirred on the linoleum and groaned. Dean collapsed by the sink.

Juanita wandered in a few hours later and woke them up. She had to warm up formula. Lazlo went to bed and Dean crashed on the sofa. He dreamt of his mother. He felt nothing.

Daddy's Got A Gun

His daddy was a stupid junkie. Little Pete used to sit on his knee and watch him shoot it in. It was cheap and easy to find back then. His daddy also took pills and drank gin and wrote terrible poetry for hours. And he liked to put on his holster and practice drawing his .45 at himself in the bathroom mirror and discuss Plato to himself out loud.

One night he was cleaning the gun and he walked into the bedroom where mama was taking a nap and stuck the barrel down her throat and pulled the trigger. Mama got real pissed off and told him to get a job or else.

Then she laid into him as to how worthless a man he was, and that if she didn't teach they'd go hungry, and how he was a goddamn cheap Romeo to every tramp in Tazewell County. She hoped he would go to Hell without delay.

Daddy stood there and slid off his belt nice and slow like a striptease and began to beat the shit out of her. And she just took it, never cried out.

Then he sat in his lounge chair near the radio in the living room in the dark, smoking a Camel and drinking from his gin bottle.

Mama got up and put on her flowered housecoat and fried up chicken and set the table. Little Pete sat there at the table not eating. All he wanted to do was run into the bedroom and lock the door.

Daddy sauntered into the kitchen finally and sat down at his plate and tossed the gun on the table along with the gin bottle. He belched and then ate four breasts without looking up or saying anything.

Then he began to cry. Loud and pathetic and wet. And mama jumped from her seat and knelt down close to him. Her eyes were bleary and they held each other. Little Pete began to howl. Daddy put his hand around the gun handle and lifted it up and shot a hole into the ceiling. The bullet hit a water vein which began to bleed down upon them.

A Stupid Night

Dean traded in his Fury on a '63 Lincoln Continental with suicide doors. He ran into Phillip at Foley's and they decided to take a spin in the new car. Dean didn't particularly care for Phillip because he was always bugging him to score powder but tonight Dean felt like having company and showing off the car.

They bought a quart of Johnny Walker and drove around. They ended up at the Bunker Hill monument and sat in the car drinking and listening to Public Enemy. The Johnny Walker bottle was almost dry when Phillip suggested that they go visit Lazlo and score. Dean was feeling generous and didn't mind. In fact, he had been waiting for Phillip to suggest it for an hour and was impressed at Phillip's willpower to not have mentioned it for close to two hours.

They made the ride to East Boston. Lazlo was

home but had nothing on-hand. He was drinking heavily. His wife Juanita was absent, but three other chicas were sitting around in tight jeans and high heels. They were also there to score and were drinking to take the edge off.

Juanita showed up with more alcohol and groceries. The females stayed in the kitchen talking and laughing loudly in Spanish, and cooked up beans and tortillas. Lazlo looked at his watch and complained that he needed a new wholesaler, that the Eye-talian that he got his powder from was cutting it too much. He was drinking gin like there was no tomorrow, which in his case, you never knew.

They all ate and watched cable sports and drank and waited. Magdelena sat next to Dean and flirted. He knew these chicas loved to flirt but didn't like to give out anything so he ignored her except to be polite. But she kept coming on to him so he suggested that they take a spin in his new car. A half hour later she said yes.

They left Lazlo's and said they'd be back in a few minutes. Instead, they left East Boston and went to Dean's loft. He had something stashed there for special occasions.

It was two dilaudid. They swallowed one apiece and Dean put on a Tackhead record. Without provocation, Magdelena began taking her clothes off.

Dean sat and watched and unloosened his belt. She stripped off everything and strutted around like she didn't care that Dean's hard-on was making its appearance in spite of his jeans. He commanded her in Spanish to come over and sit on his lap on-da-lay. She stopped her hard-to-get act and sat on him spread eagle. He unzipped his jeans and manouevered her upon him.

Elias, Dean's half brother, came home with his boyfriend Shark. But that didn't deter what was going on in the kitchen. Elias and Shark sat down and drank a beer and chatted while Magdelena gyrated on Dean's lap. They were too loaded to do anything but go through the motions. Dean got to talking with Elias and went soft inside Magdelena. She got up finally and put on her shirt and panties.

Phillip called up. He was angry because Dean had left him at Lazlo's and the Eye-talian never showed up. He demanded that Dean come back and pick him up. Dean told him that he would be over there in a few minutes and hung up the phone. Then he sat down and opened a beer. He started feeling a little queasy and went into the bathroom to vomit. A tidal wave of nausea forced him to lay down near the toilet bowl and pass out. Legs and feet came in and stepped around him to piss. He vaguely heard his name called and thought he could feel the sensation of somebody shaking him and slapping his face. Then he heard Elias say he's alright. Let him sleep.

When Dean awoke, it was afternoon and Magdelena was snoring on the couch. All the lights were on and the record player must have played the same side for ten hours. He got up and made coffee. There was nothing better to do so he read a week-old *Village Voice*.

Plastic Flowers On The Highway

The motorcycle looked like a hideous sculpture. Both rims were twisted and the saddle bent in a 45-degree angle. The headlight still worked but appeared unfocused, like a dead eye.

Blood dripped from his leather jacket sleeve. He wiped the red off his hand and face on his t-shirt and wondered if any ribs were broken. His head felt like a wrecking ball. Luckily not one cigarette broke.

He remembered about Candice. He called her name again and again. Then he stumbled over her body. He couldn't see her very well because she was thrown too far from the headlight but he knew she was dead.

He thought about walking to town but his chest and legs were starting to feel the sting. Instinct took over.

He felt around in her pockets and found the powder. He sat near the headlight and smoked it all.

Three hours passed. No one even came. Not one more vehicle passed by. It began to get light.

Even dead, Candice looked glorious. She always did love her own lily-white complexion. If only she could see herself now. She glimmered. She would be pleased.

He thought about Candice all spread out in a bronze box and ribbons draped near which read "daughter" and "granddaughter" and "niece". He could see the dirt blowing in front of the stone and the tacky plastic flowers that never rot. He even thought about fucking her one more time, because Candice would have liked that, but his body was useless.

The sun rose on the deer carcass on the pavement. It wasn't as bad a bloody mess as he imagined in the dark. Stupid sonuvabitch deer. Nothing is innocent in this world, he decided. This made him cry.

Doing Time In A Bottle

I love you. The words of betrayal. The tender kiss that becomes pain. The only men you can really trust come in bottles: Jim Beam, Jack Daniels, Johnny Walker, José Cuervo. The rest can go to hell...

Clineice poured another shot of bourbon. She fished in the ice bucket with tongs for a few cubes which she gingerly added to her bourbon glass. It's fucking Hell's kitchen tonight. Her brow glistened.

They are such pathetic creatures. Their eyes are in their dicks. And that dick is looking for another tunnel to search and destroy. Then when they have you, they try to tunnel away from you, claiming they feel trapped. Like it's all going to cave in on their head. Instead it caves in on yours.

She started bath water, letting it go as cold as she could stand it. Might as well relax. She wasn't going anywhere tonight. Getting too late. Too hot to move anyhow.

In the meanwhile, she reached for a Corona out of the ice box then cut a lime and squeezed it in. She disrobed, and holding the bourbon glass in one hand and the beer in the other, stepped into the tub and sat.

She sank down low in the water and bent her knees. They became trays for her drinks. She took the bourbon glass and held it up to the light and looked into it like it was a crystal ball.

The answers are all here. Everything makes much more sense. You can see the blind events of the past very clearly. You can understand the meaningless present. You can laugh at the sorrowful future. The demons aren't going to bring you down, at least not tonight. They're under control.

It just takes a little time and his face won't matter anymore. She wouldn't care about his chest and his eyes and his voice and his smell. It would take time but she would be set free.

She finished both drinks and passed out in the tub. When she awoke, the sun was up and her body was pale and wrinkled. This particular Sunday wasn't starting out too well.

Some Velvet Morning

She nodded out finally, her naked ass turned away from him. Dean laid back and smoked a cigarette. He couldn't get a hard-on anymore. Stupid cunt anyway. There's room for only one lady in my life, he thought rubbing his left arm.

He felt nauseous and went to the bathroom to vomit. Jesus I got to get straight. The toy has got to stop. I don't want to live like this. This sucks. Christ I'm going to be 30 in a month. I don't want to puke up another birthday like this.

He flushed the toilet. She stirred. Dean, she moaned, Dean honey. Cunt, you bore me, Dean answered. She tried to stand up but the powder had too strong a hold in her.

Dean looked at himself in the medicine cabinet mirror. He'd lost twenty pounds in the last three months.

Things aren't the same since Lazlo OD'd. And Elias got the virus and went to die in Denver. Things are moving too fast. He washed out his mouth. I'm not going to make it. I'm going to die, too. No, I got to get straight. Do that acupuncture cure. They stick needles in your ears and you don't get sick. No, all the money is tied up in product. Phone's off the hook two weeks now. Electricity's going to shut off any day. Got to pay rent. Lincoln's not running. Jesus H Christ I can't do a cure until I pay these fucking bills.

She finally got up and wandered into the bathroom. I'm sick, she said and knelt by the toilet. I'm sick of you too, said Dean, and looked at the clock. 5:33 A.M. The trains are running now. Why don't you get some fresh air and leave me alone? She had the dry heaves. Dean, I miss you, she said between gagging. Yeah, well I forgot what a wiggy chick you are. You're a real documentary case. Look at yourself. You're pathetic. I love you, she began to cry.

Someone knocked at the door. It was Gnat and Phillip. They came to buy product. Dean could always count on them. He never skimmed off their bags because they were such good customers.

Look, I'm going to bed. Don't bother me anymore, Dean said putting on a Lee Hazelwood record. I'm too fucked up to go home yet, she whined from the bathroom.

From his bedroom window, Dean watched the air lighten above the skyline. It was the only daylight he saw. "Some velvet morning when I'm straight," sang the record. "I'm gonna open up your gate. And maybe tell you about Phaedra. How she gave me life. How she made it end. Some velvet morning when I'm straight."

God Of Fast Driving

Speed. Into the arm, out into the street. Gun the motor, shoot it off. Up the vein, down the lane. It makes you feel alive for the moment and a moment is all there is left in some cases before you go back to being a piece of dirt.

But you got this car. A bone white Lincoln with a rebuilt V-8. And you scored amphetamine and you bought a whole carton of Chesterfield Kings. You've decided fuck I'm going on a road trip. And before you can catch on to yourself, you are twenty miles out of the city, flooring the gas pedal.

The whole point is NOT to SLOW DOWN. To ACHIEVE DIVINITY through EXCESSIVE SPEED. Amphetamine kicks in like STP, gives you the edge. Your neuron endings bleed into metal, chrome, rubber and plastic. You can feel every piece of loose gravel. Every tear in the pavement. Your lungs are sucking every piece of debris that hits the grille.

You can't be a voyeur behind the wheel. You have to REACT, ASSHOLE. What if something crosses the highway in front of you? What if it's your collie "Lady" you've had since you were a kid on the farm? SWERVE you say and the neuron endings swerve. What if it's your mother who ran off when you were ten and left you this stinking world? SIDESWIPE THAT SLUT you command. What if it's your brother who everybody thinks is some kind of fucking saint? HIT THAT MOTHERFUCKER. What if it's your father who drank a lot and used to throw you around? Who used to tell you that you were nothing but a jerk? KILL THAT ASSHOLE. What if it's your girlfriend who dumped you and wouldn't tell you why, then went out and fucked some moron you hate? MOW THAT SURLY CUNT DOWN.

The needle in your arm is pointing to empty so you take the service exit to a Sinclair station. You gas up and then shoot up in the Gentlemen's Room. You pull back on the highway, heading west, going nowhere. But getting there fast. Feeling godlike.

Part Two

WELCOME TO THE LAND
OF THE DROWNED

Shipwreck In A Bottle

She weaved and bobbed at the bow of the bar like the grotesque figurehead of a sinking ship. The sirens wailed tonight, luring her to crash against another vodka on the rocks. The other patrons eyed her with amusement. There is no place for a woman alone except in a brothel, a church, a madhouse.

A young merchant marine steered close and moored on the stool beside her. She tried to light her cigarette, which dangled backwards in her mouth. The merchant marine took the cigarette out, then turned it around, then stuck it back in her mouth and lit it. She looked at him in an unfocused manner then got up, knocking the stool to the floor.

"I hafta pee."

She stumbled in her scuffed white high heels to the door entitled "Gents", slamming the door open upon entry. She sat in the stall and peed for a very long time. The door opened and patent leather shoes sauntered in. She flushed the toilet and opened the stall door clumsily. The merchant marine leaned against the wall playing with change in his trouser pocket.

"Came to cheek on you."

As she tried to squeeze by, he pulled her against the wall and pushed his lips upon her neck, then her mouth. She responded drunkenly, in a semi-conscious passion, grinding her hips against his, lifting a leg and levering her foot against the sink, allowing her thighs to part. His hand swam down her dress and fingered the material of her panties. He tore them off and his cock disappeared into the wreckage. Her head loosely rammed against the door with each thrust.

When he finished, he let her down quickly and rinsed his cock in the sink. They walked out together. He continued through the bar and out the door. She buoyed herself back on the stool and chewed the ice in her empty vodka glass.

Welcome To The Land Of The Drowned

She left the hospital and wandered around aimlessly, finally entering into the tavern Aux Noctambule. Sitting heavily upon a barstool, her skirt hiked itself above the panty hose line, inviting a peepshow. She raised her drink and toasted herself in the barroom mirror.

"Here's to the ghosts of Christmas past."

She swallowed the drink and ordered another. A middle-aged entertainer with a black-dyed pompadour played sad French ballads on the accordion in the back room. A silver disco ball rotated, throwing a whirling vortex of light across the decaying faces of his audience.

A young man, not unhandsome, approached her and offered her a drink, her fifth. She turned and kissed him in the mouth deeply. He looked confused and pointed at her wedding ring.

"Yeah, I'm on my honeymoon. So what?"

"I don't understand please, where is monsieur?"

"A boring question, buy me another drink."

"You are a very mystery mademoiselle," he said offering her a cigarette.

The entertainer began playing a melancholy tango upon which she pulled her escort from his stool to the dance floor. They threw each other about in the swirling light, colliding into two old ladies dancing together. The ladies cursed at them in French. The young man fell on a chair and she fell on his lap. They began kissing deeply.

"Go to a hotel. This is not a hotel!" cried the bartender, standing over them. "You don't belong here," he said, throwing her purse at them. "You must leave now."

They got up and left, arguing with the bartender as they pushed toward the door. The entertainer smiled and winked as the young couple passed his stage. Then he threw a kiss at an ancient lady wearing a blonde wig sitting alone at a nearby table in deep reverie, tears welling in her eyes.

The young escort showed her a secret entrance into the Père Lachaise cemetery. They stumbled around in the darkness until he laid her on a tomb. He ripped her panty hose and lifted her knees so her legs surrounded him. In moments it was over. He excused himself in French and departed, kissing her on the forehead.

She laid there exposed on the tomb, feeling dizzy.

"He's part of my history now and I don't know his name," she thought, straightening up. She began stumbling around.

"Fuck him, he doesn't know mine either."

The ghosts began rising from stone, luminous to the eye. She was unafraid.

"Mademoiselle!" said a female ghost in 18th century dress. "You must not degrade yourself, mademoiselle. Your husband is new at death, he is an infant and cries to you."

She stumbled by the apparition in disgust.

"Oh sure. My husband HANGS himself in our FUCKING hotel room in FUCKING Paris on our FUCKING honeymoon and I'm supposed to be concerned about HIS FEELINGS?"

Other ghosts stopped their conversations to listen.

"I mean I'm walking around PARIS newly wed to a CORPSE. So FORGIVE me if I fuck some anonymous French ASSHOLE, at least he's ALIVE."

"Nobody gets out of here alive, darlin'." It was the dead American rock star, whose grave everyone came to see at the Père Lachaise.

"Uh gee, thanks for the meaningless cliché. I know you're a legend and everything but I think you're outta touch," she said fumbling for a cigarette.

Some ghosts tittered. The rock star smiled and without hesitation reached for her and dragged her into his arms. He kissed her deep and she did not find it unpleasant. He pulled away her blouse and kissed her breasts. They collapsed to the ground and he was upon her loosening his leather trousers, his handsome, timeless face hovering above her.

"You are a muse, dear lady, you are poetry, song and death and sorrow."

"Yeah and you're another dead asshole." She got up and straightened herself. It was dawn and she was alone.

"Uh gee, I forgot to get your autograph," she said nastily, startling a cemetery worker. He took a look at her sodden, disheveled condition. "Mademoiselle, the cemetery is closed. You're not supposed to be here. I must ask you to leave at once."

"Nobody gets outta here alive pal," she said stumbling down the path to the main entrance.

She took the metro. Morning rush hour Parisians stared at her smeared make-up and torn stockings. She pulled her trench coat closer around her.

"This place really sucks."

At St. Michel, she stumbled along the dark Seine. She stopped on a bridge and leaned over the stone rail. An eye opened in the Seine and looked up at her.

"What are you looking at you overrated sewer water." The eye blinked and continued to look at her blankly. She disrobed, stood naked upon the stone railing. A French policeman blew his whistle after her. She dove into the eye. The eye closed.

Bottled Redemption

An accomplished drunk is someone who is lonely. Of course, anyone who sets out to be good at something staggers down a lonely road.

She practiced drinking and became good at it. She came to New Orleans 20 years ago to die, but it was taking longer than anticipated.

Sitting near a headless angel in the cemetery off Basin Street she had already drunk herself into a sad sublime, when the sky suddenly and quickly darkened, ready to pour. She rose to leave and coughed blood as she staggered toward the entrance. To her horror the black iron gate had already been padlocked shut for the evening. Clutching the bourbon bottle, she moved unsteadily down a row of tombs and fell against a large granite cross. She leaned on the cross for balance. It was strong and rugged like a man's shoulders. It felt safe. She wept bourbon tears.

Johnny Virgo sensed he was dying. The knife had gone in deep three times before he could get a shot at the prick. Who would have thought a cracker Circle K store clerk would know how to stick someone like that? The prick not only made him drop the paper bag of money but he also punctured Johnny's lucky Rock of Ages tattoo: a beautiful, long-haired girl embracing a stone cross in a turbulent sea. The girl's hair bubbled blood red on his back.

The sirens ridiculed him. He scaled the plastered cement wall that enclosed the cemetery, leaving bloody handprints on the new whitewash. A heavy wall of rain descended unmercifully upon him. He limped down a row of tombs and came upon an old woman crying on a cross. She seemed familiar somehow and he stumbled toward her. *Rock of Ages, let me hide myself in Thee.*

"Holy Mother, protect me," he murmured and collapsed dead at her feet.

She looked up from her crying stupor and imagined she saw a beautiful, young, handsome angel of death with the whitest skin and the blackest hair and the wildest eyes. He knelt down and kissed her feet tenderly.

"Kind and gentle lady, I will never abandon you," he said. She smiled. The bourbon bottle slipped out of her hand.

"I've been waiting for you so long at the bottom of this bottle," she addressed Johnny's collapsed body then laid next to him. Together they formed an island surrounded by quick-moving rivulets of blood, bourbon and rain.

Salvation Is A Last Minute Business

The bitch had seven pups before Mrs. Seelye remembered to have her fixed. And they all turned out ugly like their daddy, a stray blue tic, not collie like their mama.

"Just my luck, just my luck," Mrs. Seelye muttered under her breath while grading fifth-grade math papers. "A worthless husband, a nasty child, and now the dog's been spoiled."

She called her husband to stand before her.

"Now you take that deer rifle and purge my sight of those mixed pups. And bury them deep so the bitch don't dig them up."

"No don't !" It was their ten-year-old daughter Penny. She grabbed on to her daddy's legs as he walked toward the gun cabinet.

"You mind your p's and q's little missy. Now go to your room this instant or I'll get out the yardstick," chirped Mrs. Seelye crisply.

"I don't care, I don't care. Don't kill my doggies, daddy!"

"Little girl, you best do what she says and go to your room. I promise I won't let your doggies suffer," said Mr. Seelye, petting Penny's head.

"I hate you! I hate you! I hate you!" Penny ran away.

Mrs. Seelye slammed down her papers. "Now will you look at that. I sweat and toil trying to teach ignorant brats all day and I have to come home to more impudence. I swear the Lord gave me too much to handle, between you sitting around all day useless, and her sass. My reward had better be sweet."

Mr. Seelye looked at her with glassy eyes and said nothing as he loaded the rifle and walked out slamming the screen door.

He opened the shed door. The collie bitch looked up at him, her newborn pups squealing and writhing on her belly. He paused for a minute then leaned the rifle on the wall.

"Hell, don't need no bullets."

He pulled the pups away from the collie bitch and

put them in a pile. The bitch growled low but did nothing. Then he pulled off the shovel from its hook. He stood there poised to slam the shovel down on the mound of pups when the bullet knocked him off his feet. He couldn't get his breath, and blood pumped out of his lung. He looked up to see his young daughter cocking the rifle and pointing it at him.

"You say you're sorry."

Mr. Seelye couldn't speak. Then it went black.

The screen door slammed. Mrs. Seelye yawned and continued to mark up papers with a red pen.

"You done already? I hope you didn't track up the floor."

The blast ended up in her belly and knocked over the chair she sat in. Papers scattered, graded with blood. Mrs. Seelye's glasses fell away leaving her blurry. She couldn't feel her legs. A steady and growing agony built up in her belly. In the blur, she saw her Saviour and heard His voice.

"Say you're sorry."

She smiled up at Him, then frowned quizzically.

"Sorry for what?"

You Always Shoot
The Ones You Love

Mama recalled that it started with the nanny goat. Daddy bought it for us children, but one day he came outside from a nap and saw nanny goat on top of his new Firebird. Nanny goat disappeared. We cried for three days, walking around the meadows looking for nanny.

Then there was the white rooster we raised from a chick. One morning Hamlet stood on top of the air conditioner outside the master bedroom. And he crowed for the first time as a man-rooster. Daddy hadn't been home but three hours from pulling a drunk with some buddies from work.

Mama fixed up chicken for Sunday dinner. We children just looked at our plates, not knowing for sure why we didn't want to eat the meat except that we wished Hamlet would come back from vacation, which is what Mama told us.

In the summertime just after dusk, the bats would dart back and forth, in and out of the trees surrounding the house. Daddy would sit with his rifle on a lawn chair and sometimes hit one. Then there was an old hoot owl that lived in the gigantic oak tree twenty paces directly in front of the porch. It was minding its own business. But it was not wise enough to avoid daddy's bullet.

There were squirrels, rabbits, doves, deer, sparrows, snakes, moles, fish, red foxes, stray dogs. One time he bought an old bear from the zoo and shot it because he heard that bear meat was a delicacy. Instead, it ruined all of mama's frying pans, and the more you chewed, the larger it swelled up in your mouth so it was impossible to finish a bite without choking.

One late night in the spring, the eldest Dixon boy, Henry, pounded on our front door waking our family up. He pleaded with our daddy to go help calm down his brother, Bobby. Henry explained that Bobby Dixon was real drunk and had their mama and daddy locked in a bedroom and was threatening to kill them and himself with a foot-long hunting knife. Daddy grabbed his Colt and he and Henry ran down the block.

The lights were all off in the Dixon house and,

from the first step into the foyer, the house reeked of grain alcohol. Henry yelled up the stairs to see if his mama and daddy were all right and that he had help. Bobby yelled down that he was going to kill them all and that they should all say their Hail Marys.

Daddy spoke loudly and calmly to Bobby that he should come down and talk this thing out. Bobby moved to the top of the stairs and spit back that he didn't want to talk and that daddy better go home or die.

Daddy started walking up the stairs real slow, coaxing Bobby to just calm down and drop the knife. Henry stood at the bottom of the stairs and didn't utter a word. He let daddy do all the talking. They could hear Mrs. Dixon crying on the second floor.

Daddy pulled the hammer back as quietly as possible as he proceeded up the stairs. Bobby became more agitated as daddy approached the second-floor landing. Then he laughed hysterically and charged daddy on the stairs. Daddy had no time to think. He pulled the trigger and Bobby Dixon's head exploded.

Daddy had to sit at the county sheriff's all night, filling out papers and answering questions over and over again. Finally he was released, dismissed from any thought of foul play.

The incident shook something up in daddy. He

had never killed a human being before, not even in WWII. He started drinking morning, noon and night for a month. He talked and argued with himself, with the dead boy for hours on end. Finally, he took his gun rack and buried the whole thing, guns and rifles and all, near the oak tree.

And all the animals came back eventually, as if the gates to Eden had been miraculously left open.

Squirrel Hunt

Harley Grote carried the .44 inside his suitcase rolled up in a T-shirt. He handed the suitcase to the Continental Trailways attendant, who put it underneath in the baggage compartment, and carried on the fruit and cake basket his mama gave him.

Every Grote in Andalusia showed up to the station to wave him off, forty-some-odd Grotes in all. About two dozen ugly female Grotes came up and kissed him on the cheek. Harley was the seventh Grote to go to college, but none had made it out as yet, they either flunked or quit. But the Grotes came from a stubborn seed, and there was no doubt in their minds that Harley would bring their name to glory. From his seat in the back he dutifully waved to the shining, ugly, happy faces.

In Montgomery, Harley changed the ticket from Tuscaloosa to New York City. He left the fruit and cake basket in the men's restroom. His bus came and he got on.

He fell asleep immediately and dreamed black and white about him and his daddy hunting in the woods for deer but all they could scare up were squirrels. They sit around the porch skinning the squirrels. The skin comes off like a fine glove peeling off a hand. A dozen squirrels lay side by side, clean and gutted, their decapitated heads and tails in a pile near their feet. Then she comes down to supper with just her bathrobe on, his cousin Tammy. She slips off her bathrobe and sits naked between him and his daddy. Mama passes around the black-eyed peas and the cornbread, then the fried squirrel. And daddy says Tammy get on the table, I'm hungry for pussy. And Harley says no don't you touch her. His daddy picks her up and sets her on the table. Harley picks up a dinner knife and stabs his daddy in the stomach. Mama starts yelling and Tammy buries her head into Harley's shoulder. His daddy sits back down and laughs and says well, if she means that much to you the hell with it. And mama smiles and Tammy kisses Harley on the mouth.

When he stepped off the bus at Port Authority it was early morning and chilly. He put on his bright orange hunting vest and hat and wandered in a southeasterly direction carrying the suitcase. His orangeness became a magnet to every steely bum on the street and Harley silently gave a dollar to anyone who asked. By the time he reached Tompkins Square Park he was near penniless.

In the park, tent city was rising. The bums dusted themselves off and replaced their cardboard and blanket tents into their grocery carts. Harley reached down for a stone and focused on a squirrel foraging on the ground. The stone left his hand like lightning.

Harley picked up the deceased squirrel by the tail and walked over to a group of bums standing around a barrel fire. He expertly skinned the squirrel and pierced its carcass through a stick then laid it over the flame.

A group of young crusters sat on a park bench drinking morning beer. A girl cruster with faded green hair and a nose and lip ring walked over to the fire.

"God, that's so cool. Can I try some?"

Without comment he handed her the sizzling carcass. She took a bite of it and fanned her mouth.

"Wow, this is really really cool. I think you are really interesting and I want you to meet my friends."

She took his arm and dragged him to the bench. Three disheveled youths eyed Harley with boredom.

"Hey, we're having a cookout."

"Oh really?" asked a young man in dreds, rolling a joint in his filthy hands.

"I want to roast marshmallows. You have any money?" the girl asked innocently.

Harley nodded and brought out the last of his money, about ten dollars. The cruster girl took it and walked toward Avenue B.

"I'll be back in a little while."

Harley sat on the bench. After an hour, the three youths left. He sat there the rest of the day, and when night came he rested his head on his suitcase and slept on the park bench.

He dreamt his mother was rocking him, then she abruptly left the room. He could hear muffled arguing. His father's face appeared suddenly big and close to his, smelly with sweat and alcohol. Harley couldn't move. He began to cry. What we got here, a little sissy? His father began rocking him violently.

Harley fell off the bench just as a bum tugged at his suitcase. He jerked the suitcase back and the bum slid down the bench, swearing. He snapped open the suitcase slightly and felt for the hardness of the .44. The rest of the night he sat in vigil, one hand around its handle.

For a fortnight, Harley wandered the East Village. At noon each day a church set up tables at the park to feed the bums, so he ate. Sometimes people came up to Harley and tossed him money as he sat shabbily dressed on Avenue A. At night he slept in the park, hidden up in the fork of a tree.

One morning without warning, dozens of police in riot gear entered the park. They stood guard as sanitation workers threw the bums' makeshift cardboard tents and meager possessions into waiting garbage trucks. Protesters entered the park with makeshift banners. An old man bum waved a dirty teddy bear in the faces of the police standing ominously in formation. Someone threw a brick, hitting an officer. Police armed with nightsticks began pummeling on sight. Within moments the park was in pandemonium.

Harley roosted on a limb, hidden from view. He pulled out the .44 and aimed randomly. The shot went unnoticed.

"Hey, this is so great, a fucking riot." It was the girl cruster climbing toward him. "What are you doing, killing the pigs? That's so cool."

Harley looked down and saw his whole ugly family. He shot his mama in the stomach, his father in the head. He shot his sisters and brothers, his aunts and uncles.

He reloaded the .44.

"Can I shoot somebody?" The cruster girl reached for the gun. Harley saw his cousin Tammy and pushed her out of the tree.

"Get out of my apple tree you whore."

The cruster girl rubbed her bloody knee angrily and pointed up at the tree.

"Sniper! Sniper!"

The park evacuated except for the dead and the wounded. The police barricaded the park. TV trucks with satellite disks outnumbered the police wagons.

"Throw down your gun," boomed a voice through a loudspeaker.

Harley tossed the gun and shimmied down the tree. The sky took on a sudden storm darkness. He walked toward the police-lined barricade with his hands above his head. As the police handcuffed him, reporters with microphones and video cameras swarmed around him.

"What was your motivation to gun down people today? Was it to protest kicking the homeless out of Tompkins Square Park? Are you an anarchist? Do you belong to any terrorist organizations? Are you part of the PLO? Is this to protest the bombing last week in Northern Ireland? Are you a white supremacist..."

The reporters hushed as Harley shook his head. A thunderclap came out of the east. Camera flashes and video lights haloed his sandy blond hair.

"Naw, I just hate people," he said, and climbed into the police wagon.

The Deluge

It was as if it had rained forty days and forty nights, but in reality it had rained hard and deadly for only three. Along the levee the water level raised fifteen feet and had already flooded out the lower areas. It felt like God was trying to kill everything off and start over again, like the time her big brother, now deceased from pneumonia, drowned the newborn kittens the calico bore and chased it off, too, with his BB gun out of meanness.

Evelina flipped through the pages of the movie magazine and cut out the picture of a handsome dark-haired youth with a brooding smile. She pinned him on the wall next to various other pictures of Hollywood stars above her bed.

"If you ain't the stupidest girl I know I don't know nuthin'."

Her mother, Mrs. Pickett, stood in the doorway

drunk on Everclear and bitterness.

"An ocean in the backyard and you sitting like a goddamn bump on a log," she slurred. She entered the room and swayed over Evelina.

"What makes you think it does you any good to tack these loverboys up? They don't want you. You ain't going nowhere," she said ripping down a picture.

"I hate you and I'm going to run away," Evelina hissed.

"Suit yourself you little curse. You know I don't mind none if you drown. But you got chores."

Mrs. Pickett grabbed Evelina's arm and hair and dragged her out off the bed and down the hall.

"Leave me alone. I'll kill you," Evelina screamed at her mother.

"Leave me alone, I'll kill you," Mrs. Pickett mimicked and slapped her hard on the face. Then she lunged at her daughter's breasts, as if to tear them off.

"You drunken pig, get off me," Evelina screamed and punched her mother square in the stomach.

Mrs. Pickett stared down upon her daughter with the demon look. Then she hesitated. Her eyes widened and she gurgled as if the Saviour Himself was choking her, and fell sideways dead.

Evelina stepped aside her mother and in her fright

knocked over the hurricane lamp. Flame chased oil to Mrs. Pickett's clothes and lit up without complaint.

Evelina ran out the door to the barn and propped open both doors. The '52 John Deere tractor, unattended since her daddy ran off with a secretary, started with little trouble and she drove it into a wave of rain down the waterlogged country road.

The river ran red from Georgian clay. At the one-lane truss bridge the river rushed even, washing on to the roadway. She drove upon the bridge at full throttle. The structure jerked and collapsed from the additional weight and red water rushed through the railing, submerging the tractor. Evelina screamed and fell into the current. She went under but quickly clawed her way up for air, the current sending her quickly downstream. She went down again and swallowed water. An arm grasped her and she imagined she was being rescued.

She opened her eyes underwater and found herself wrapped around a partially decomposed corpse. The strength of the current popped the skull off its neck-bone and it disappeared into the redness.

Evelina climbed to the surface and gasped, coughed and screamed at the same time. Coffins from an uprooted cemetery bobbed around her like a fleet of rudderless ships.

She held on to the handles of a cypress casket and rode down into a clearing, what was once Turpin's Hollow. She floated with the casket alone on the River Styx undecided on which bank to paddle to.

She sunk deep inside herself and imagined the rain had ceased and the clouds parted. The sun appeared and a rainbow stood ahead down the river. She imagined her mother spoke to her kindly, and asked for Evelina's forgiveness. Her father appeared and tearfully apologized for abandoning her. The movie star with the brooding smile swam up next to her and kissed her gently, whispering to her to marry him. She imagined the red river to be the blood of the Saviour, and she felt cleansed. She was swimming in His blood, this river a vein to glory.

Dead Horse

Most people in Goofy Ridge, population 300, didn't know what heroin looked like in a person. Everyone thought Dwayne used needles and acted sluggish because he had diabetes, so it worked out quite well indeed. And in a little backwoods fishing resort where there was a tavern for every dozen adults, they were too drunk to care anyway.

He took the drive up to his dealer in East Peoria on a Wednesday night. Traffic was clean so he made it up there in good time, maybe 30 minutes.

After Dwayne purchased the usual, he pulled in to the truck stop on Route 9 and shot up in the bathroom. Then he sat at a booth and ordered a big meal, which he couldn't eat by the time it came. It sat there as he stared out of the picture window.

Up drove a Chevy pickup hauling an equestrian

trailer. It parked toward the back. Two men jumped out and ran to the back of the trailer. The trailer shook like it was possessed. The gate gave in from the pummeling of hooves. It shot out like a white god, an albino stallion.

One of the men grabbed the loose reins and jerked down on them. The stallion reared and tried to crush the human's skull. The man dropped the reins and rolled underneath the truck. The other man shouted something and ducked behind the trailer.

The stallion trotted around the parking lot, head and tail high, laughing. It galloped down the service road and went full stride into highway traffic.

Everyone in the truck stop ran outside. The horse reared up on the blacktop. Cars screeched and skidded into the vehicles ahead of them. The horse bucked down the middle of the road laughing. A Peterbuilt semi hauling hogs to slaughter saw the horse too late. The driver laid on the horn but the horse stood up and laughed in its face.

The truck jackknifed and rolled over on itself, sliding to a stop covered with blood and viscera. Screaming hogs fled the overturned trailer. A hog began feeding on the mangled horse. Stunned passengers wedged out of their vehicles, car horns froze in disharmony.

For hours Dwayne laid on a grassy knoll overlooking the flashing beacons of the police and tow trucks. He felt the wings of his high subside and shrink into his back. He smiled and lit a cigarette. Life never felt more godlike and meaningless. His head fell back to the stars to see the constellation Pegasus laugh down on the earth.

Purgatory Has A Body

She wandered bar to bar through the Quarter killing sailors, which is the superstition if you light a cigarette from a candle. Into her second pack of dead sailors, she finally found him sitting at a row of video poker machines playing Deuces Wild next to an old man.

She ordered a scotch and watched him lose. He was just as she remembered him: young, handsome, tall and lean wearing a white undershirt, baggy trousers and sporting a straw fedora. He was her Other.

He finished the game, picked up his beer, then walked up and leaned next to her at the bar.

"I forgot how you smell like jasmine," he drawled, smiling at her. "It's nice to see you, Eurydice."

"Is it?" Eurydice took a sip of her scotch. "It seems to me you forgot a lot of things, Orpheus. Like fetching me from Hades for instance."

Orpheus's eyes followed a girl with long legs walk across the barroom.

"I've been busy."

She pounded the scotch glass on the bar. The bartender looked over at her.

"I gave you beauty and a purpose and you were supposed to come get me. You were going to take me away from that horrible place. That was the deal. That was your part."

He gave her a shit-eating grin then took a long swallow of beer.

"Yeah, well, it's a new world and love is dead. I don't want to save you or anybody." He eyed the girl with long legs bending over the cigarette machine. "And as for beauty, I find it in lots of faces these days. Besides, you got away. You didn't need me."

"You're wrong!" she spoke loudly. Bar patrons glanced at her. "We're part of the same poem. We're bound to each other!"

"Sorry, sweetheart. I don't write those songs anymore. I like my immortality sunny side up." He placed the empty beer bottle on the bar, tipped his hat, belched, and walked out the door whistling.

Eurydice sobbed and shook. The old man walked up to her and patted her gently on her back.

"There, there. Where's your husband, miss? He better come get you." She pulled away from the old man annoyed.

"Did you ever sail a boat?" she said pulling out a cigarette.

"Yes miss, I was boatswain's mate in World War Two."

She lit the cigarette from the candle.

"Then you're dead."

The old man walked away, shaking his head. Crazy young girl coming in here all drunk, talking to herself at the bar and crying, making a spectacle. He was just trying to be nice. He sat back down at the row of video poker machines and inserted a dollar.

Life Is A Slow Death

She threw his belongings out the back door. The pile lay there under a sheet of plastic and boards. He just covered it and left, books, clothes, everything, and left.

She smoked a cigarette to the end looking at the pile from the kitchen window. She hasn't seen him in a couple weeks now. Why the hell doesn't he just come and haul it all away? Then they wouldn't have to look at each other again. She crushed the cigarette into an ashtray.

No, he wants an excuse to come back, she thought, and he wants to torture her a bit. She should throw it all in the street for pick-up, she smiled.

The phone rang, third time today. She answered and again somebody hung-up on her. It's been going on for a few days now.

It was one of those gasoline-meets-its-match

attractions. Fast and hot and drunken, and now a slow, agonizing death that was lasting longer than the initial flame.

They were drunk on red wine the night he told her he wanted to start seeing other girls. He might as well have slapped her, kicked her in the stomach. She knew it was coming, somewhere deep inside her knew it was coming, but it was still a shock to hear the words out loud and naked.

"Let's go shoot pool," she slurred.

They rode bicycles in silence to a tavern in the Bywater. He walked straight up to the bar and she sat down at a table. He brought her over a red wine and picked up a pool cue.

"I challenge you to a duel to the death," he smirked, inflecting like Mickey Rourke's character in the Bukowski movie *Barfly*.

She drank the wine down like a shot and stood up defiantly.

"Stop talking like Henry Chinaski, you are annoying me," she said and stumbled to the table.

He broke, and a stripe ball went in the pocket. She swayed drunkenly as three more stripe balls went in one by one, then a scratch. On her turn, he leaned over close to a girl in zebra pants and whispered in her ear.

She hit the cue ball with a drunken velocity and two solids raced into a side pocket. She glanced sideways to see him caressing Zebra Pants' arm. Her stick slipped and the eight ball rolled into the corner pocket.

"You win, killer."

She left the cue stick leaning against the table and walked out the door. She was unlocking her bicycle when he came out after her.

"What the fuck are you doing? Where you going?"

"I'm going home so you can make misery in Miss Zebra Pants' life."

He spread his arms innocently holding a beer bottle.

"What, what? I'm just having a little conversation. Nothing to get excited about," he said in Henry Chinaski inflection.

"Go to hell," she said crying.

"Baby," he put his arm around her. "Come back into the bar. Baby," he said, smiling smugly, "I'm not worth it."

She erupted into tears and sped off on the bicycle. As she pedaled down the barren street she cried hysterically. "It's over it's over it's over."

"Stop your fucking bicycle!" He caught up with her.

"Stop and throw your bicycle down!" he ordered. She stopped her bicycle and threw it down on the street. He did the same.

"You're taking this all way too seriously," he said, lighting a cigarette. "It wasn't going to last between us, so why are you acting so maudlin?"

"You're a cocky sonuvabitch and I'm not going to stand here while you justify your shallow existence to me," she said while taking a piss behind a parked car. "I care for you and I want you to care for me. Don't torture me. Don't even pretend you feel nothing for me."

She picked up her bicycle. A black boy walked up and flashed a revolver.

"I want your money," said the black boy pointing the gun at the drunken couple.

"You're interrupting a very important conversation," she said angrily.

"Say, is that a .38?" he inquired of the black boy in Henry Chinaski inflection. "It's a nice-looking piece."

The black boy stared at the crazy drunk white couple. After a long silence, he spoke up.

"It's a .32." He put the gun back into his jacket and disappeared between two houses.

They looked at each other and started laughing. She took off quickly on her bicycle, leaving him there in the street.

"Stop right now!" he raced by her. She stopped and flung her bicycle on the curb.

"You're not just going to ride off into the sunset like that on me," he said, dropping his bicycle and walking toward her. "I do care about you. Maybe too much. But all love is a tragedy. Even if we got married and grew old together, one of us would eventually die, and that's tragic." He stopped before her. "I don't want to fall in love with you or anybody. So, cut the crap. Let's go home and watch a movie." They stared into each other's eyes.

"I don't know who's the bigger fool," she said, finally.

That was the last time they saw each other. The phone rang. Again, the other end hung up. It's him.

No, it's some girl trying to track him down, she thought sadly. Somebody will always be there to pick up his pieces. He's a charmer. But she has to do all her dirty work. She shifted in the chair and lit another cigarette.

"Life is a slow death," she said aloud. The echo in the kitchen agreed with her.

A Bus Named Cemeteries

The sky had that sad look. It had been depressed and close to tears for nearly a week. Finally, the sky broke down and cried. It wailed hard and long and wet like at a good funeral.

The river bloated and climbed up the levee, threatening to bleed over into the Quarter. The rain was a nuisance, but he was glad it washed away the sweltering July heat.

What is life? he thought, rolling another cigarette while staring out the window from his kitchenette. A good bottle of gin, he answered himself. He lit the cigarette and took a drag. The smoke appeared to float around the Beefeater bottle like a genie making an appearance. There's no wishes in this bottle here, he thought to himself. A fifth of gin and an occasional girl to have some laughs with, that's the best you can hope for.

He came to New Orleans seven years ago with the intention of becoming a professional drunk. You have to be good at something, and he figured it was destiny as he had three kidneys.

Try as he might he couldn't think of any one event in his life that was tragic. There was no dark shaded past, no lost love.

In fact, he grew up regular on a farm in Indiana. Nothing in particular pointed to that he would throw himself into a river of gin and tonics.

Around three in the afternoon the squall subsided and he wandered into a bar in the Marigny. He drank and played pool for an hour when a messy red-headed girl in white sunglasses stumbled into the bar and immediately tripped on herself. She sat loudly on a barstool and ordered a red wine. As she dug in her purse for money, the sunglasses slipped off her nose and fell on the floor. She lifted the glass of wine and immediately spilled it on herself, staining over the heart.

He watched her with interest and chuckled at her clumsiness. She wore only a slip, as many bohemian French Quarter girls did in the summer, and he admired her legs. She walked heavily in high heels to the jukebox and played Chet Baker. Nobody played Chet Baker in this bar except for him. She began dancing to herself drinking her wine.

He became transfixed with this girl right out of his dreams. He aimed and broke the rack of balls with a thunderclap. She looked out of her stupor and met his eyes and walked directly over to him.

"Can I use you?" she asked. Her eyebrows were penciled in dramatically and her large eyes gave her the appearance of a silent screen actress.

"Sure. What do you have in mind?" he said smiling, leaning on the pool cue.

"Let's get a bottle. Let's get lost."

They stopped at a deli on Decatur Street and bought a large bottle of red wine and a couple of shot bottles of gin and proceeded up the street toward Canal.

"Let's pretend this is turn-of-the-century New Orleans when there were still streetcars named Desire and I'm a Storyville whore and you are a criminal in exile," she said swigging the bottle of wine.

"I like that. What kind of criminal am I?" he said.

"A killer."

"You're a strange girl."

He held out his arm for her to hold on to. They cut up Toulouse to Bourbon Street. Drunkenly they careened past strip clubs, sex and trinket shops and loud bar music.

"Now let's be weather. What's your favorite storm?" she asked.

"Twisters."

They became tornadoes and whirled up Bourbon, bumping into boring, annoying tourists and laughing hysterically.

At Canal, the Desire bus sped by, out of their reach. They boarded the very next bus, which read Cemeteries as the destination, and drank all the way to Metairie. The bus stopped at the complex of city cemeteries and they stumbled off.

They entered the closest cemetery across the street and staggered around giggling and kicking each other.

"So who are we now?" he inquired.

"We are Greek gods," she said passing by a pantheonesque tomb.

"Then I'm Dionysus, god of gin." He opened a shot bottle of gin and drank it down.

"And I am Melpomene, muse of tragedy," she said, then tripped, collapsing on the grass.

"What are you so tragic about?" he said holding out his hand to pull her up.

She ignored the hand and looked at him. Her large, saturnine eyes welled up and reddened. He sat down next to her.

"I'm sorry. It's the wine," she drawled slowly.

"No it's not. Now tell me why it's so goddamn necessary to cry."

"To wash away the bad. But it just gets all bad again."

He sighed impatiently.

"You know everybody's got bad to deal with. You can't take it all so seriously. It's not worth it. When things get me down I take a swig and turn the page and forget it. That's how I stay on top. Girls, jobs, nothing is worth getting so down."

He pulled her to him and tried to kiss her. Her lips responded sluggishly. He looked at her and frowned.

"What's up with you? I thought you were my Storyville date?"

Her eyes rolled in her head and her head jerked down.

"I'm tired right now." She leaned against him heavily.

"What's wrong with you? You passing out on me?"

"I took some pills." she mumbled, closing her eyes.

"Well, give me some."

"Sorry, I took them all."

"What do you mean?" He nudged her. "What do

you mean you took them all?" he spoke loudly.

"I just get so tired of dying," she murmured.

He shook her, then patted her face strongly.

"I'm sorry I used you. I just didn't want to die alone." She fell forward into unconsciousness.

He stood up in horror and twisted around wildly. He ran out of the cemetery leaving her there, and entered into the world of sorrow and uncertainty.

Hole

You are attracted to the hole in his head. Those lips. You have to have those lips closing in on yours. It's the only thing that matters on this earth right now. You can't help yourself. You stare. He catches you staring and likes it, you can tell. He's probably an asshole but that doesn't matter. No, that makes it all the better. You can treat assholes mean and not feel so bad. You can be yourself. Life is getting pretty shallow. As shallow as your whiskey glass. He orders you another.

Together you leave the bar and go to your place. Smoke a cigarette. Do Jim Beam shooters. Talk trash. Repeat the same old incantations. His name is Richard. Richard the Lionheart. Richard the lying heart or something like that. Baby baby, do your personality striptease. He's looking good even if he is married and an asshole. He's occupying time. He's getting you through another hour. Shallow company is better than the black hole of your own. Smoke another cigarette. You like his earring but don't care for his tattoos except for the purple broken heart on his chest. Wounded in action. Maybe he has some soul after all. Maybe you're the one who doesn't have soul.

You climb aboard and it's like riding the saddle horn of a bucking bronco. The ride lasts ten minutes. When it's over, he gets up and dresses. He falls on you lying there and kisses you tenderly, one for the road. You smile. You'll never see him again and it feels good and bad.

The Heart Is A Lonely Prey

Eleven eleven P.M. She stumbled toward the railroad tracks that separate the Marigny from the Bywater, swinging a bottle of spirits nearly empty as her own.

"Quiet as a tomb, quiet as my tomb," she coughed and spit.

At the tracks she sat and fumbled for a cigarette. Somewhere, in a shotgun dwelling a hundred paces away, her latest beloved was in the arms of another, an old phenomenon but always startling nonetheless.

"What a joke. I hope they are very hippy together. I hope they are very hoppy together. I hope they are very heppy together. I hope they are very—" The warning lights flashed on and the caustic horn of a lone engine intruded into her sorrow.

She stood and stared into its bright eye as the engine emitted a litany of piercing epithets. She threw off her jacket and shook it at the train like a petulant matador.

"Toro motherfucker!"

At the last possible moment she stepped forward and felt the wind from the engine passing behind her. Black is my heart, black is my heart, the wheels and pistons sang in unison as the engine disappeared into the dark again.

Death clapped his hands and stepped out of the shadow. "Brava, Manolita."

"Spying on me again? I'll call on you when I need you." She lost her balance and dropped her jacket, leaving it on the grass.

"My child, my only thought is to escort and assist you in any way."

She stumbled on to Royal Street and swayed into the Bywater.

"Yeah? Well I want to shoot guns with Hemingway and get shitfaced drunk with Baudelaire, and I want to die a loud glorious death with some beautiful boy screaming my name."

"Ah a poet" sighed Death, "so sadly missed by those who scorned him to death. It's a wonder and great privilege indeed to be present in some five-dollar flophouse and witness a Great Soul's death throes. To witness a Great Poet, penniless and derelict and alone, his Great Heart misses a beat then another and another."

"Shut up."

They wandered a block past Piety Street to Desire then turned toward the levee.

"My dear child, I hope you're not on this bender over some sniveling love affair."

"Fuck you."

"Let me chance a guess. He kissed you tenderly in the garden like Judas kissed Our Lord, then as the cock crowed three times, like Saint Peter he turned around and callously denied your existence. And presently he's taken fancy to the lips of another who hasn't nearly your heart, soul, beauty and talent. Am I close?"

"Go away."

"I can tell you right now, if it's any consolation, that it won't last between them. In fact they are arguing as we speak."

"I don't care. What are they arguing about?"

"Something to do with the television. Not very poetic. But then again most muses are not very poetic or remarkable. Most muses, when it comes down to it, are quite ordinary and boring. Take Dante's childhood muse, Beatrice. She grew up to be somebody else's housewife and quite uninteresting. You'd never know that from his descriptions of her."

They came to the corner of Desire and Chartres. Beyond the levee wall a barge churned on the Mississippi.

"I wanted you to see this ship on the river. Would you care to join me?" She shrugged and he lifted her gently and carried her over the threshold of the levee wall to the river.

A barge indeed was passing by, heading down river, luminous from a multitude of souls waving to her from the decks. A small rowboat floated away from the barge toward the bank.

"Would you like to come aboard? Baudelaire and Hemingway are dying to meet you."

She hiccuped and frowned.

"I feel sick. I want to go home now." Back on the street she swallowed the last drop of liquor, and dropped the bottle on the street. The bottle rolled toward the curb, crescendoing like a drumroll.

"Bitch."

Three young black boys on bicycles flew quickly like ravens toward her.

"Bitch, how much, bitch, how much," chirped the ten-year-old.

"How much for your booty, bitch," sang the thirteen-year-old.

She walked silently up Chartres. The eight-year-old darted his bike close behind and grabbed her ass.

"Give up your booty, bitch." They circled and stopped in front of her path.

"Fuck you." She kicked the ten-year-old's bike out of her way. The eight-year-old brought out a .38 and aimed it at her head.

"I'll kill you white bitch, I kill you."

She twirled around wildly, looking. The eight-year-old fired four shots in succession. She fell painlessly. The three boys disappeared, leaving her lying alone on the street.

Death jumped off the levee wall, and walked up to her and sighed, then leaned down close. She gurgled on blood, her heart missed a beat, then another, then another.

Marilyn Monroe Died Miserable, Too

She spoke to no one as she drank five bourbons at Lafittes. Near midnight she stumbled out on the street and walked up a few blocks to Rampart and entered the door which flashed TATTOO. A young man with tattoos covering both arms watched television behind the counter.

"I want a shipwreck on my chest."

The young man eyed the drunken middle-aged woman swaying at the counter with bored interest.

"That'll be one hundred fifty dollars, ma'am."

The needles were not an unpleasant sensation. The ripping flesh didn't compare to the hairshirt she wore around her soul. It felt even good, almost.

Two hours later the S.S. Titanic appeared to be

sinking into a sea of blood between her breasts. She walked out of the shop still half-drunk, which meant she was still half-sober, and so hurried to another bar in the Quarter to continue her drowning.

Within three bourbons straight-up, she lost her balance on the barstool. An ugly boy helped pick her up and bought her another drink. He seemed too young to be an ex-marine, though that's what he claimed. He began talking about getting shot at in Lebanon, laying behind sand dunes hearing bullets striking the sand around him. This perilous image interested her and attracted her to him and despite his homeliness she consented to leave with him.

They were walking through an abandoned parking lot when he kissed her. He tasted like a carton of Viceroys and stale bottle beer. He laid her down on the gravel and hiked her skirt up. She was too drunk to feel anything.

And as he continued to drive into her out in the open on the gravel, and as the sky began to lighten towards morning, that's when she noticed the famous glamour queen smiling down upon her from a casino billboard. That's when she began thinking about Marilyn Monroe.

It's just that you'd think she had enough beauty

and charm to get what she wanted. But she fucked up just like the rest of us ugly sons of bitches. She really blew it. And somewhere, like it's written, we're supposed to feel like it was a bigger tragedy, that her tragedy was more beautiful than our own. Well, how much lower can you go than six feet? The fact of the matter is that her bowels stank up her lonely deathbed and by now worms have eaten that Mona Lisa smile right off her face.

This thought made her laugh so hard that the boy stopped and rolled over, looking puzzled, and the Titanic tossed and shook violently in the ocean waves.

Inside A Hurricane

She sat up at the bar and crawled inside a hurricane. The sickly sweet rum concoction traveled up the straw and passed between her maroon painted lips.

She waited for the click to go off in her head, for the moment of dead calm, for the point of no doubt. Three hurricanes later she was still waiting restlessly and so she took the fourth to go.

It was a warm and windy October afternoon and she wandered down to the river. She waited as the Algiers Ferry docked on the New Orleans side.

"Weather channel says that tropical storm's in the Gulf," she overheard two businessmen walking on the ferry. "I surely hope it hits Pensacola," they joked.

She leaned over the railing on the top deck and stared down at the velvet green river. She entertained the notion to jump into the velvet and creamy foam, to drink river water cocktail until her lungs ruptured and her heart burst. She imagined herself all ballooned out from death, half eaten by a hundred river creatures, washed up on the bank. Instead, her eyes welled up with melancholy and her throat choked on sadness.

"I have forgotten how to die."

The ferry docked and commuters exited. She sat and waited for the trip back across river. A young navy boy and his fiancée and mother sat near her. The young man put his arm around his fiancée as his eyes followed two blondes walking by. His fiancée slapped his knee playfully. He yelped and laughed and tickled her.

"Behave, son," said his mother shaking her head.

The boy leaned on his mama and kissed her.

"Aw now, I'm getting married in less than an hour and you'd begrudge my last few minutes of bachelorhood?"

The ferry pushed off the Algiers landing and blew its horn at an approaching barge. She couldn't help staring at the young couple. In her world hope could be dangerous, but the couple's innocence astonished her. She felt a sense of envy and even relief that maybe there were happy endings after all.

The young man stood up and handed his bride his navy cap. He grabbed the railing.

"Did I ever show you this trick?"

He hopped up on the railing and flipped up into a handstand. His mother stood and gasped loudly. The ferry shook in the wind and the boy fell backwards off the railing into the lacey foam. In horror, mother and fiancée ran to the railing. The boy disappeared under the hull.

An unearthly howl turned the heads of the other commuters and even the mother and fiancée, to see a woman with eyes turned inward, crumpled and writhing on the deck, arms flailing, as if tossed by something unseen. The sound came from somewhere deep inside of her, like a desperate communication from one drowning soul to another.

Ophelia Descending

She dressed at midnight and walked into the Quarter. On Decatur Street, young punks sat in doorways laughing and drinking, and Bourbon Street vibrated like a decadent carnival.

She passed a young couple kissing against a wall and it embarrassed her. It shamed her to be alone, though the thought of meeting someone new and falling madly in love seemed so remote, impossible. To fall in love with another face, another body, to hear another story, to reveal her story all over again. It seemed too exhausting, too...

She wandered down to Cafe Du Monde and sat down for a coffee. Still, she searched the men's faces, looking for the next one, the next lover, but none intrigued her. When the coffee arrived, she lowered the cup below the table and poured in bourbon from her purse.

"Happy anniversary darling," she toasted the ghost at her table. "I knew I could count on you to show up at my darkest hour." She drank the cup quickly.

"Nothing matters. No, it's chance that matters. It's not giving a fuck that matters. It's a certain degree of selfishness that matters. You are nothing unless you think otherwise."

The ghost shook his head sadly.

"I'm so jealous of you."

She leaned over and filled the empty coffee cup with bourbon.

"You'll never grow old or lose your beauty or become a washed-up joke like me." She accidentally flipped a spoon off the table. The ghost let it lay.

"If you don't buffer yourself you'll be beaten down. You'll slide into quicksand. And if the people you choose to love do not love you back, you will sink. And you will grow weaker, and crazier."

She examined the ghost. She had forgotten the mole on his neck. He died in a car accident many years ago. He had broken their engagement and run off with another girl. They cracked up the Buick in Mexico.

"Go away. You've condemned me to myself."

Billy watched her every move. He had been

watching her for months wandering around the Quarter but hadn't had the nerve to talk to her. Though she seemed a lot older, he was drawn to her pale and fragile beauty. She seemed not of this earth. She was always alone and that added to the mystery.

She arose and knocked over a water glass in her drunkenness and left the cafe. He followed her down the street. The downers he took earlier had taken complete effect and he caught up to her. Up close, her hazel eyes had a world weariness and sorrow and it scared him, but he persisted with downer courage. He took her hand and gingerly kissed it.

She looked at the young man with astonishment. He looked so young, a gutter punk with red eye-liner and torn leather jacket. Something told her not to take back her hand, not to send him away.

"How long hast thou been a gravedigger?" she said coyly, smiling.

Billy looked puzzled and glanced away momentarily.

"May I walk with you?" He put his arm out for her to hold on to. She paused drunkenly then placed her arm through his. They walked silently down the sidewalk.

"How old are you?" he asked as they turned toward the levee.

"It feels like I've been shipwrecked on this lesser star for five thousand years."

An empty barge quickly and silently floated upstream. They walked down the steps to the river and sat, dangling their feet off the dock.

"I think you're really beautiful, a goddess."

She began to shiver. He took off his leather jacket and put it over her shoulders. She brought out her bourbon and handed it to him. A man with a fishing pole appeared near them and threw out the line. They drank the bourbon silently as barges floated past them. The fisherman left and they were alone on the river. He turned her face to his and they kissed.

"Mortal love, what tragic fools it makes of us," she said sadly, "but I'm grateful for this illusion, even if it's temporary." He put his arm around her and they watched the air lighten into morning.

"Hey Billy, where the fuck you been, asshole."

Three gutter punks ambled down the steps toward them.

"We've been looking for you all night," said a boy with four nose rings. Billy quickly rose, grabbing his jacket from her shoulders. The morning light betrayed her eyes. The girl with blue hair glared at her then crossed her arms.

"What the fuck are you doing Billy?"

"She's just a friend. Don't go crazy."

Billy looked down on her. "I have to go now. It was nice talking to you." He and his friends walked toward the Quarter. The girl with blue hair took his hand.

"What were you doing kissing her for? She looks like a corpse."

His face darkened. "She's not like that. She's a nice lady. I felt sorry for her." He paused. "I feel sorry for you, too," and he tickled her. They began to wrestle and push each other down Decatur Street, laughing.

"The king is dead!"

The strains of an early morning jazz funeral sluggishly proceeded down the street as she numbly walked home.

"The king is dead," repeated a dark old man leaning on a cane.

The brass band somberly marched like rusty tin men, one step then another step, playing a funereal dirge. Mourners followed, stepping gingerly down the street as if in a trance, waving parasols adorned with ruffles and ribbons. A horse-drawn glass hearse passed by carrying a white casket.

Once home, she dressed in the wedding gown her mother had made for her, twenty years old now and unworn. She had kept it in a box all these years like a secret. She pinned pink silk roses in her long auburn hair and closed the door to her apartment behind her, not locking it.

At the Andry Wharf she crossed the streetcar tracks and walked onto the dock where the freighter Propertius sat moored. She boarded and walked across the deck to the river. Two crewmen hurried toward her with coffees in their hands.

"Ma'am, where the hell are you going?"

She climbed over the railing holding the train of her dress.

"Hey Joe, she's going to jump!" Three more crewmen appeared and rushed her.

She crossed her arms and fell forward into the river. The dress spread and floated around her. A life ring landed and she pushed it away. She floated with the current as the crew yelled and scrambled on the deck, peering down upon her. She froze in the November water.

The dress and the fierce undertow soon weighed her down and her head went under forever. At first she struggled, holding her breath. She heard a tympani drum roll, or maybe it was her heart. The drum roll crescendoed as she sunk deeper in the murky water. She opened her eyes and the tympani became deafening. It stopped abruptly and cymbals crashed. Her eyes stayed open.

you have just read
angel with a criminal kiss
a creation book
published by:
creation books
83, clerkenwell road, london ec1r 5ar, uk
tel: 0171-430-9878 fax: 0171-242-5527
creation books is an independent publishing organisation producing
fiction and non-fiction genre books of interest to a young, literate
and informed readership. your support is appreciated.
*creation products should be available in all proper bookstores; please
ask your uk bookseller to order from:*
turnaround, 27 horsell road, london n5 1xl
tel: 0171-609-7836 fax: 0171-700-1205
non-book trade and mail order:
ak distribution, 22 lutton place, edinburgh eh8 9pe
tel: 0131-667-1507 fax: 0131-662-9594
readers in europe please order from:
turnaround distribution, 27 horsell road, london n5 1xl
tel: 0171-609-7836 fax: 0171-700-1205
readers in the usa please order from:
subterranean company, box 160, 265 south 5th street, monroe, or
97456
tel: 503 847-5274 fax: 503-847-6018
non-book trade and mail order:
ak press, po box 40682, san francisco, ca 94140-0682
tel: 415-923-1429 fax: 415-923-0607
readers in canada please order from:
marginal distribution, unit 102, 277 george street, n. peterborough,
ontario k9j 3g9
tel/fax: 705-745-2326
readers in australia and new zealand please order from:
peribo pty ltd, 58 beaumont road, mount kuring-gai, nsw 2080
tel: 02-457-0011 fax: 02-457-0022
readers in japan please order from:
charles e. tuttle company, 21-13 seki 1-chome, tama-ku, kawasaki,
kanagawa 214
tel: 044-833-1924 fax: 044-833-7559
readers in the rest of the world, or any readers having difficulty in
obtaining creation products, please order direct (+ 10% postage in
the uk, 20% postage outside uk) from our head office
a full colour catalogue is available on request.